JOSEPH BOYDEN

Wenjack

HAMISH HAMILTON
an imprint of Penguin Canada,
a division of Penguin Random House Canada Limited

Canada · USA · UK · Ireland · Australia · New Zealand · India · South Africa · China

First published 2016

www.penguinrandomhouse.ca

*This book is a work of fiction. While incidents in the novel are based on real people, events,
and locations, they have been recreated fictitiously. All other characters, dialogue, and
events are the work of the author's imagination and are not to be construed as real.
Any resemblance to current events or locales, or to living persons, is entirely coincidental.*

LIBRARY AND ARCHIVES CANADA CATALOGUING IN PUBLICATION
Boyden, Joseph, 1966–, author
Wenjack / Joseph Boyden.
ISBN 978-0-7352-3338-6 (paperback)
ISBN 978-0-7352-3339-3 (electronic)
1. Indians of North America—Ontario—Residential schools—
Fiction. I. Title.
PS8553.O9358W46 2016   C813'.6   C2016-904595-1

ILLUSTRATIONS BY KENT MONKMAN
DESIGN BY CS RICHARDSON
PRINTED AND BOUND IN THE UNITED STATES OF AMERICA

10 9 8 7 6

WENJACK

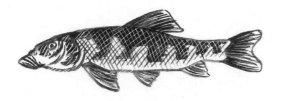

SUCKER FISH

Gimik-wenden-ina? Do you remember? I remember, me.

My friends, the two brothers, call the pale teacher Fish Belly or sometimes Sucker Belly. They don't say it to his face because he's strong and he smells like what the colour yellow or maybe brown smells like, and he has a room in the basement that scares the life from us. He calls me the slow one. Even though they took me away from my home two years ago when I was nine I am still in the first class but Fish Belly says I get to go to a new class soon. I'm learning my English, me. But I won't lose my tongue.

I pretend to be the slow one so I don't forget my words. When the Fish Bellies with shining shoes and guns tied to their waists came to take me, Nindede said not to speak my words out loud but only to whisper them when they couldn't hear. Daddy. Nindede. Mama. Nimaamaa. My sisters. Nimiseyag. My dogs. Animoshag. I will see you again, yes? Indian. Anishnaabe. If the Fish Bellies hear me speak my words they beat me with a stick and make me eat soap.

Tonight is the night they line us up and then we climb in the water tub, two, or three of us if we're real skinny, and we have to wash the back of the one in front. Then we get out and Fish Belly rubs each of us with a wet towel. This means tomorrow is prayer day. I can tell which niijii, which friend, ran away from the school this week by the long red marks on his back. Ever a lot of red marks. Ever a lot of friends who ran away this week. But Fish Belly teacher has Fish Belly friends who go out and catch them. We have a secret path, but maybe it's not so secret anymore. The Fish Bellies are good at catching Indian children. One day I will run. One day they won't hurt me anymore.

CROW

The three boys didn't plan to run away
from the school on that October afternoon. But the sun was warm enough that
they took off their windbreakers and tied
them around their waists, and it was the
older of the two brothers who said to his
younger sibling and to Charlie that they
should go visit an uncle who would take
them out on the traplines so that the
school people they called Fish Bellies

would never find them again. A dozen children had run away from the school that week but all had been captured and returned and beaten.

The three boys made that impulsive decision on that Indian summer afternoon as boys are wont to do. They climbed the fence when they knew no teacher would be looking and disappeared like thin ghosts into the thick forest of spruce and poplar and willow. The two brothers covered ground quickly, walking fast then slipping into a run, pushing each other the way brothers who have nothing else but each other do. They didn't get upset when they had to stop and wait for pigeon-toed Charlie, placing thin red willow shoots into their mouths and chewing on them, squatting

6

on their haunches and staring wordless at the forest ahead, their eyes carving the path they would soon take.

Near the secret path that the children used to sneak away from town without being seen, Charlie found a discarded railroad schedule with a route map in it. He hoped this might serve as a guide to his home and carefully folded it and put it in his thin jacket's pocket. Charlie had a lung infection. Tuberculosis and similar diseases had taken thousands of Indian children's lives the last years in these strange schools, always built with a cemetery beside them to bury those the attendants knew would not make it to the final grade. Charlie had once shown the two brothers the long red scar that began at his collarbone then arced down and split his chest before curving off to his back. He'd been opened up by a white doctor's scalpel as a child but when the brothers asked him why, he claimed not to know or even to exactly remember how old he was when the scar was made. On this bright October afternoon, the sun beginning to fall and the cold beginning its wind through the black spruce, Charlie coughed and spat phlegm, his breathing a whine. When he caught up to the two brothers, no words were exchanged nor any judgment or anger as the two boys rose from their haunches and bounded off into the growing darkness, Charlie following as best he could.

How do we know this, you ask? We watched them. We, those who chose to, took the form of crows and followed them silently and swiftly, swooping by them then hovering above before diving down to land in the branches of dying trees to stare upon them, our cobalt eyes sparkling to absorb the last of day's light.

HUMMINGBIRD

Ever glad my friends wait for me. They go fast and disappear in the bush and I have to look careful as I follow for ghosts of footsteps or broken twigs they leave for me or the thin paths through trees that I know in me are the ones they take. I need to stop and sit and when I do, nenookaasi, a hummingbird, comes near my head and stares at me, so close I hear her tiny wings hum before she flies away.

That is a good sign. I know it.

Getting dark and I can hear something following. Is it the Fish Belly men? My body won't give me enough breath to run like my friends but I try anyways, and every time I catch up they stand from squatting and spit the twigs from their mouths and disappear again.

But now dark is almost here and I hear the Fish Belly teacher word. Don't. I catch my friends finally and my inside chest burns and I spit some red-and-white spit on the ground but this time they don't stand and disappear again. I kneel beside my friends and we huddle for heat and don't say anything but glance into each other's eyes then look just as quick away. We all say the same thing without saying it out loud. Go back now and get switched but don't get real cold tonight. Or get real cold tonight and wait for light but don't stop running to where we run. None of us wants to go back even though we now understand how cold the night is going to be. We are going to stay anyways and my inside chest begins to stop hurting as bad. Don't hurt, chest.

The older brother reaches into his jacket pocket and pulls out some toilet paper and the other brother reaches his hand into his own pocket and pulls out some dry grass. I reach into my pockets and feel the map. I will need this. I feel bad when my hands come out empty to say I have nothing. The older brother reaches into his other pocket and pulls out what looks like a little stick and holds it in front of him, showing it to us in the shadows like it is something we need to pray to. I lean closer. It's a match, but even in this little bit of light I see that the blue head of it misses its red tip.

The two brothers gather dried twigs and then I watch as they kneel to the ground, their heads almost touching as they work with their hands. The older one takes the match and they both whisper and then he picks up a small stone and runs the match across the top of it. Nothing. He does it again. Nothing. The third time he does it I hear the match snap and then the ko ko ko of an owl somewhere not far away. The brothers say Gaaaah! and then laugh quiet and sit down on their bums.

I know what Owl says when he says ko ko ko but I don't want to tell my friends and scare them. Instead I tell them I saw a hummingbird and it's a good sign for us, but the younger brother says no, it's not, because they were all supposed to leave at end of summer and if one is still here it will die of the cold.

The brothers get up and we walk to a big black spruce and snap its lowest bottom bits off and make a bed for us under it from the green smell of it. That smell makes me want my home and my nindede and my sisters and dogs. The brothers whisper and one hums a bit of a radio song, and then I listen, my eyes open and staring up through branches of gaa waan dag, of spruce, as both begin to breathe like waves coming onto the beach with their breath of sleep. So dark now under the night and clouds that hide

stars and moon that I can only hear the
mouse chewing on the toilet paper and
dry grass and dried twigs from our fire,
the fire that couldn't live. I'm cold. Cold.
Nin giik aj. Ningiikaj I whisper as I flutter
like a hummingbird to sleep.

I wake from hard shakes and in the
darkness feel like I'm all by myself until
the clouds pass, and in the light of Giizis
moon I think I see an owl above watching me and when I turn my head slow I
see the brothers curled together. Slow as I
can I move closer to them and slow I curl
as close to them as I am able and soon we
are three curved sticks floating on the
back of a great and rough and freezing
river that carries us and swallows us and
carries us again toward the sun morning.

OWL

When darkness comes, some of us who
follow the three boys descend from bare
tree limbs to become mice. Those of us
who choose this form sniff then gnaw the
twigs and paper the children have left as
offering. We sit on our haunches and we
hold this detritus in our tiny paws and
watch with twinkling black eyes the three
brown children buffet along the swollen
rivers of sleep, their bodies clutching each

other for warmth.

Those of us in the trees above who choose to stay perched instead shift into owls, twisting our heads and blinking our slow yellow eyes to refract the moon and stars' light to sight. We twist our heads to one another and call out ko ko ko, whisper to the children below, then swoop on silent wings with talons spread to pierce the mice and carry them squirming above. We perch on limbs and look down at the shivering children as we swallow the mice whole, their tails twitching in our beaks as we watch the one called Charlie awake and look up at us before crawling closer to the two brothers, searching for warmth.

Charlie. His real name is Chanie. But the ones who forced him to that school can't pronounce or don't care to listen and so say it with sharp tongues instead. If we could feel pity for this one, we would. His walk before, his walk to come. Neither is easy. All he wants is home. We follow now, we follow always, not to lead but to capture. Someone, yes, will capture this boy's life.

As the coldest part of North October night sets in, we who are owls gag and retch. We've absorbed the essence of our captive mice and now cough up their bones and fur. We spit what we can't keep down to the boys below, not in contempt but in honour. Nothing. Ko. Nothing. Ko ko. Nothing, ko ko ko, should go to waste.

Just look at what these three boys do. They've left the hissing radiator's warmth, a dormitory bed, night floorboards creaking under the weight of those charged with their protection. These boys, and the dozen children the week before them, have all run away for a reason. But these three, these three will go further than the others. They are driven.

We stare down upon what they can and must live through. They shake in half sleep despite holding on to a friend or a brother. When they awake, though, they will feel the shame of having touched one another, if even just for warmth. This lesson not taught by their own but by others will by morning dissipate with the early frost. Alas, we get ahead of ourselves. The school these three were dragged to will continue to call to them like distant shouts through the poplar.

And these three, Chanie especially, will try to concentrate on the choked breath in his ears as he runs, the whine in his lungs, his inside chest burning.

We who choose to be owls watch all this, blink our yellow eyes slow and cough down pellets to the three boys below. The fur and bones won't keep them warm. But the one truth we know is this slow blink of our own yellow eyes. These children we reflect in our retinas will awake at least one more morning. They will wake staring into the black of the centre of our eye and will rub their own and make sunspots, the yellow orb of light growing rounder to pull them from the ground to go.

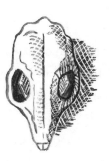

MOUSE SKULL

I wake up, me, to the older brother staring
down. The sun rises behind him so that
light shoots from his body. My arms are
wrapped around his brother with his back
to me and we are curled like dogs. I watch
as the older brother shakes his head in a
big no. He kicks the younger one hard
who cries awake. I suddenly feel guilty.
The older brother turns and walks to the
path and squats on it, looking away. The

one beside me jumps up and says Ever stupid, you! Then he kicks me, too.

I crawl up on my knees and then push my hands on the ground to stand up straight. My knees feel like what an old man walking looks like and my side is hot from the tip of the boy's shoe. The younger one has joined the older and both squat and chew on sticks and stare down the path they will take. I want to walk to them to be friends again. I don't know what I did, me. The air between us is cold and heavy and sparkles with sun morning. Giizis.

I walk in a small circle with my eyes to the ground and let the circle get bigger. This will warm me and let me get closer to them, too. Under last night's tree our green bed still holds the shape of our bodies. I stop in my circle and look up at the tree losing its leaves that kokoko stared down from. My eyes go to the ground and I see now what he left. I pick it up in my hands and run a finger along the hard and soft of it, this cough-up shaped like an egg, and this thought makes my belly rumble. My fingers pick through it, pull it apart, the fur and little bones of waa waa big on oojii mouse. Waawaabigonoojii. Ever big name for such a small one.

At the centre of the ball of fur and bones my fingers stop picking. Careful as I can, I remove the bits of fur that still stick, and then my fingers pass to my palm a perfect mouse skull. I hold it up to the sun morning and through the glow-ing eye hole I see a shining black pebble, tiny and sparkling. I bring the skull closer and smile at my find. A tiny black stone stuck where Mouse's eye used to be. This is beautiful. I will give it to the brothers to say sorry for what I don't know I did, but when I turn to walk to them, I see that they are gone.

I'm hot again when I reach the brothers squatting and chewing sticks, the mouse skull safe in my jacket pocket with the map. This is all I have but this will be enough for now. My inside chest burns and I spit some red on the ground as I lean on my knees and try to breathe good. The brothers don't look at me as they rise to run, and I don't feel bad. I can feel they are no longer mad at me for what I don't know I did. I think they don't know, too. I will give them this gift when we stop and rest proper. I will give them the most perfect thing I've ever found because they wait for me and they care.

The forest begins to open up as the sun looks down from straight above. I can tell, me, we are getting near a big river or maybe a lake, the ground leaning to it now just a little bit. I've been good at knowing which way the brothers run. I'm not so scared anymore in the sunlight. Not so scary in the day. Gii zhi gad. Giizhigad.

I can tell which way they run because they go the way that's easiest to make. Sometimes there's more than one choice but if I look close they leave me messages of a broken bit of willow chewed up so the red skin of it shows the white meat underneath. When I find them, I pick them up and put them in my pocket so I have something to prove to my friends I knew they were close. That I am here, too.

Every little bit when I need to rest, I reach careful in my jacket pocket and take the gift even more careful in my fingers and peek at it for just a second. The light of Giizis touches the black pebble eye and waawaabigonoojii mouse winks at me. Today is okay. Today there will be no school.

The trees are bigger here. The ground leans harder. I'm closer now to water. I can no longer run, me, but walk fast instead and let the slow hill carry my body. Thirsty. Water soon. The Fish Belly who teaches us doesn't let us drink any water when we answer words wrong. He doesn't let us eat, either. I'm used to hungry, me. But I can't get used to no water.

I can hear a river now, and soon see its bright back twinkle at me through the azaadi poplar as Giizis sun touches it to say ahnee hello.

PIKE

We flick our amber tails and torpedo
through the tannin-stained river, gills
breathing water as we gather into flashing
schools before, in ones or twos, we depart
our company to swim alone. One of us
takes the form of northern pike, yellow
eyes with sparkling retinas searching for
sustenance and finding a young pickerel
hiding behind a shoal on the riverbed.
Short chase before the lunge, needle teeth

clamping, this fish small enough to be gulped in two torn swallows.

Rising to the shining surface now and exposing back and dorsal fin to air, we laze in the last of the season's warm sunlight, wide mouth open and drawing water along scalpel teeth, gills flushing it out in a heartbeat rhythm. Our yellow eyes stare into the dry world above, poplar and black spruce shimmering up the bank. The weather will change. It will change by this time tomorrow, carrying first winter on its spine.

We see the one named Chanie emerge from the trees and limp pigeon-toed toward us, breathing hard. We move closer with a swish of tail so that we may watch him fall to his knees by river's edge, his face above a shiver in his dry world. His hands enter the water pale palms first, and then he merges the whole of his head into our wet domain, eyes closed as he gulps and gulps, lifting his head back out to breathe before sinking it back in to drink some more. Poor boy is so thirsty he forgets his father's lesson to never drink this way but to drink with cupped hands instead.

We laugh at Chanie's forgetfulness and that's when he opens his eyes underwater to stare into ours, catching a glimpse of us peering at him, amused. He startles and pushes himself back up and onto shore and so we flick our tail once more and cut along the bank, hugging it for a distance to where we know the uncle of the two brothers has built his weir. We will offer them a small gift today because we see their hunger, especially the smallest boy's.

We enter the weir of rocks that merge into a V, the channel we travel narrowing to the uncle and his long stick and snare, our head entering the circle of wire as he deftly yanks the long stick with his strong wrists' flick, the wire tightening across our throat as he lifts the pole above him with us flopping in the noose tied to its end.

The uncle carries us writhing in our stranglehold up the bank to his small cabin. He wishes we were bigger, for his two nephews have appeared ghostlike from the trees, which means two more mouths to feed. But alas, we are just a young pike. He will use every bit of us, though, his wife especially, who will boil even our head and sharp ribs down into a stock.

Uncle sees when he reaches his camp a third young one now, a strange boy with wet black hair plastered to his forehead, and wonders how many more children the forest will birth. Another mouth to feed when his autumn hunt has been so unsuccessful is one mouth too many. He worries us from our noose and lays us belly down upon his plywood table, takes his thin and sharp fillet knife and, pinning our head with one hand, slices with a long draw of wicked sharpness across that place where skull meets spine.

We shiver convulsions when he severs us from life and wriggle free from that coil just as the uncle whispers miigwetch and opens the pike's mouth to place a small tuft of tobacco upon its tongue. Invisible on the wind now, we rise up to the

poplars and tussle the dying leaves,
rattling them in an honour song to one
more day of life for those who gather
around the blood- and scale-dappled table
to watch this man prepare their meal.

SPIDER

I can see it's the same fish, me. It's the
same giigoo, his eyes cloudy now on the
table and he doesn't look so big. But that's
him. I saw him with my head under the
water. I went in his world and saw him.
The nimishoome of my friends, he presses
the fish's neck with his knife, and me
and them, we step up closer to watch.
Nimishoome cuts the back of giigoo so it
can stop moving around on the table and

then he takes some cigarette from his pocket and sticks it in giigoo's mouth. I swear, me, that when the nimishoome does that, the fish sticks his tongue out at me and whispers Gaaah! And then its open ear on the side closes for the last time and wind in the azaadi trees starts to hum and moan.

A girl and her nimaamaa come out from the little cabin behind us and stare at me until I look back at them and they turn their eyes to my two friends. Lots of people here. Ever lots. Too many for such a small fish. My two friends. Their uncle nimishoome and his girl and her nimaa-maa. How many is that? I count them on each finger with my other hand in a whisper mouth.

Bizhig. Niizh. Niswi. Niiwin. Naanan.

When I'm done, I see the nimishoome looks at me before he moves his eyes back to his shining knife turned red. I look back at my hand, at my fingers, and see none are left for me. What is my word for none? I bend each finger to meet my palm and when I'm done counting again I know this family has no skin for me.

My friends push closer when their nimishoome slices the shiny sides away from giigoo and then his top too and lays the meat on the table. Then nimishoome turns him over to remove his insides. The long white stomach and bright heart and brown guts spill and I watch the shining knife slit open the white and out flops two parts of a smaller giigoo fish the bigger one had eaten. The nimaamaa comes up then with her bowl and scoops it all inside then turns and walks, her daughter following, into the dark mouth of their home.

In their cabin I watch nimishoome and his wife make sure we young ones have some giigoo and a bit of fried potato and hot fish water in our cups. A lantern hangs above the table and I think I'm the only one who sees asabikeshii spider weaving in her corner of the cabin, the lantern making her web sparkle, a small bug like a dried leaf caught in it. The two who aren't children don't eat so we can and I am so hungry when I'm done I wish I could eat my plate. Nimishoome scrapes what is left from the pot onto his wife's plate and she pushes it back across the table to him and he pushes it back to her. I take the rest of the fish water in my mouth and go from the table so I can lie by the fire in the woodstove and watch these people be a family. The girl who is so quiet watches me and doesn't take her eyes away when I look at them. Ever good looking, her. My eyes can't stay on her she's so pretty. She sticks her tongue out at me and I smile. She's lucky the Fish Belly ones who found me haven't found her yet to take her away to school.

Nimishoome tells his nephews their story instead of eating. He puffs on a pipe so the smoke makes his face go soft and he tells them the story of how their nindede, how their nimaamaa, both died near the train tracks. He doesn't tell them this story to make them sad but to let them know they aren't alone. I didn't know till now that the brothers have no parents. All they have is this man, their uncle, this woman, their auntie, and this girl, their cousin. Nimishoome tells the boys the story of their parents, the boys listening at the table with their mouths open, so that they know they still have family.

I move closer to the stove because the floor is cold tonight. My nindede and my nimaamaa and my sisters live near the train tracks. I will walk to them so we can be a family again. I reach in the pocket of my jacket as I listen to the uncle talk and watch the asabikeshii spider sitting like a grandmother in her web, listening also to the stories that the uncle tells, and I feel for the map in my pocket and run my fingers over the skull of the mouse. My eyes are tired from the smoke but I am warm and not so hungry and listening to the hum of the uncle's words makes me feel as good almost as if I am home.

Nimishoome talks and smiles as he watches his wife eat till she is full but then his soft look turns hard when we hear something outside. Each of us quiets to listen. Feet coming to the door and then the door crying open and I see the same Fish Belly man who came to take me away from my family standing big in the door, his boots like a black mirror and a gun tied to his side. His mouth opens to take the pretty girl away and I reach to stop him and wake to the dark cabin now except for the hot light that creeps out of the stove and someone has put a blanket over me and I am finally warm. I'm warm. The Fish Belly man is only a bad dream and I listen to the wood crack in the stove beside me and I feel like this is safe. The Fish Belly man is not coming for us. He has lost our path and he won't find us because we are better in the woods than him.

I reach in my pocket and take out the map, and in the jumping light of burning wood in the stove I unfold it and look at the lines that run across the paper and try to guess which way I will go. I can't see her, but I know that grandmother spider watches me careful from the world she made from her body, wondering too which way tomorrow I will go.

WOOD TICK

We weave our web in the corner of the
trapper's cabin and watch as young
Chanie falls asleep by the woodstove.
He's as close to content as he's felt since
his last night at home two years ago, the
night before being taken away by the
pale strangers. He falls asleep not with a
full belly by anyone's measure but at least
not one that feels gnawed from within.
We take no pleasure when we share that

this is young Chanie's last warm night.

Chanie awakes to the uncle stirring the fire in the stove to life again. It's still dark but Uncle is up and preparing a journey. We watch from our web with our many glittering eyes as young Chanie stands from his sleeping place on the floor and tries to be helpful but doesn't know what to do. The only thing the school he's run away from has taught him is how to be fearful of adults.

I saw the giigoo we ate last night before you caught him, Chanie says to the uncle. I saw him underwater when I put my head in to drink.

The uncle doesn't understand this young boy. He understands the words, the Ojibwe weaving through the stubborn English. He fears the boy carries a burden

that will kill him. And the uncle doesn't
want this curse passed on to his family.

The uncle brews bitter tamarack tea,
for it is all they have to drink this morning.
When its scent awakes his wife she
comes to him and he whispers in her ear.
I will take our nephews today up the lake
to the trapline. We will go a week. You
stay here with our daughter. Eat from the
last store of food.

The aunt shakes her head.

Don't worry, the uncle explains. We
will come back with something to eat. We
have no other choice.

It's not the food, the aunt says. She
looks to the boy who sits by the stove
and stares into it at the shimmering
light, the light out the window beginning
to come.

Your job is to send the stranger away, the uncle says. Someone broke something in him. We don't have tools to fix it. Send him back to the school. Or find out where he lives and send him there. Give him a little food for the journey.

The uncle rouses his two nephews and they climb from their shared bed, rubbing eyes and standing. They pull on their thin jackets when they see Uncle head to the door. Chanie stands, too, and finds his own jacket. When he joins them, the door open now, the uncle turns. Four will be too dangerous in my canoe. We head north on the lake and I can see the weather's changing. He walks away, the two boys following. None of the three look back to Chanie. It isn't their way.

The girl lies in her bed and stares at

this strange boy. She can see something in him, she thinks. Someone hurt him bad. Ever bad they hurt him. So bad that it is stuck inside him and he's so scared of it but more scared to let it out. She watches as the boy sits back down by the fire and she thinks she sees his shoulders quiver. She watches as he reaches in his pocket and takes something small out and studies it before he places it back in. And then he pulls out a piece of paper and traces his finger along the lines sketched on it. He folds the paper and puts it back in his pocket and stands. He sees she stares at him but she won't move her eyes. She dares him with her dark eyes to tell her why he hurts.

I'm going outside alone to play, the boy says, then walks to the door. Quick as we can, we secrete a single silver strand of gossamer from our abdomen, spinnerets crocheting to drop us down from our web and onto the shoulder of the boy as he passes through the door.

We ride him to the edge of the woods to a bed of dried leaves where he drops to his knees and begins to cry so hard his shoulders shake us from him. He buries his face into the leaves so that the girl and her mother won't hear. The wails slow to sobs slow to hiccups as we shiver the last of the leaves above him, separate leaf from branch and drift down to him as small offering that we watch. And so that he can't shake us from him again, some of us turn into a wood tick and crawl up from this bed of leaves and latch ourselves to his calf.

When all the tears have left his body, Chanie walks with something as close to certainty as he knows. He's made a decision. He will follow his friends and their uncle by land to the camp and make himself useful so that the uncle will like him. And when Chanie's chest has healed some and he has earned some food to take, he will then begin the long walk down the tracks to home.

Inside the cabin he tells the mother and her daughter that he is ready to begin his journey home. Although it isn't a lie per se, Chanie knows to leave out that first he will find his friends and their uncle, but still this makes him feel wrong. The girl's mother explains the path he needs to take to the railroad tracks and where the path divides, how he must turn with the river rather than follow the lake to where her husband's trapping cabin sits.

Chanie nods and the mother wraps a few pieces of dried moose meat in waxed paper and places it in his pocket. Remember, she says, when you get to the tracks you must go this way back to the school. She takes his right arm and holds it out from his side. If you go the other way, she says, you will have too much bush to walk. She drops his arm. Which way do you go at the tracks? she asks. Chanie lifts his right arm from his side.

He looks to the mother and then to the girl. He walks to the door. The girl reaches him before he leaves and slips into his palm a small screw-top glass jar that holds seven matches. These will keep you warm at night, she says.

Chanie puts the jar into his pocket, his finger brushing the little mouse skull. He takes it out and places it on his palm and presents it to the girl. This is the most beautiful thing I own, he says.

She stares at it. Waawaabigonoojii.

Take it, Chanie says.

She holds it up to the sun in the door and smiles when the black eye of us winks at her.

He travels most of the day as we gorge just a little on his blood with our tiny fangs' pierce, and when he reaches the place where the path divides, he steels himself and hurries along the lake as best he can, reaching the uncle's cabin by mid-afternoon. But no one is there. Chanie sits on the step and waits, staring out at the lake, an east wind rippling it, the wind cold. Weather will change, and it won't be good.

Chanie takes out the jar of matches and can see his reflection just a little in the glass. He daydreams what it would be like to see the girl's reflection in it too. He curls up in the last bit of sun on the shallow rough porch, dark clouds skittering. He doesn't know he's been sleeping until the footsteps awake him. The uncle stares down at him, a look of surprise on his face. The look turns blank again and Chanie peers through the man's legs to see his two friends squatting a short distance away. They watch, red willow sticks in their mouths.

You can't stay here, the uncle says. You must return to the school. Look, the bad weather approaches and I have no room for you. Stand now and begin your walk back.

Chanie stands as he's told.

When you take the path that will get you to the tracks, the uncle says, you turn this way to your school. He lifts Chanie's right arm from his side. Don't forget. If you travel quick, you will beat most of the weather. And if you see one of them workers on the track, you ask him for a bit of food.

The uncle walks into his cabin, and the two friends stand from their crouch to follow. When they pass Chanie, each reaches a hand out to brush his left arm.

BEAVER

Push out of the forest to where the
straight and shining lines they built cut
through my world. I stare, me, at these
tracks. It's that time now when day wants
to become night but wants to stay light,
too. I can see the sun smiling as it leaves
through the white legs of azaadi poplar
and the furry arms of gaawaandag spruce.
Sun winks at me from the way I'm not
supposed to follow the tracks. From my

other arm that will lead me back to the school the sky has turned the colour of a fire after it's dead. Ash snow and its cold is coming from that way, and maybe it is sent to me from the teachers at the school, from the men the colour of a fish belly who hunt me to take me back. They won't find me. I won't let them. I won't go back to that place.

I walk up on the little rock hill that holds the long straight lines. Ever long when I look each way. Ever long. The wind blows cold from my arm where the school lives when I turn that way. It makes me hold my skinny jacket closer. When I look the way my nindede and my nimaamaa and my two nimiseyag live, where they wait for me, I watch the last sun set the two steel lines on fire. I think of my nindede, of what he would say. Eat. Don't make decisions with no food in your belly. Think of your nimaa-maa and what she wants for you.

The strips of mooz soften with spit. I don't want to but swallow all the mooz down to make my belly feel better. Shiny paper that held it fits my pocket. I will keep it. It will find its use. The wind gets harder and cold up here on the tracks and outside of the trees. Which way? Nin-dede's smile when I walk through our door. My two animoshag barking and jumping on me with wet tongues. My two nimiseyag laughing till we cry. Whispering to my nimaamaa that I am home now and she cries till she laughs. Follow the sun. There is no choice. I must walk till the sun comes back to push me from behind again. My two friends touched my other arm for a reason. They said to me loud as they could to not go back to where we ran from.

The map asks me to look at it to make sure and so I do. The wind shakes it and it almost sounds like the map wants to talk to me. I think I have it turned the right way. I've watched older people study maps and I do what I remember them doing, running my finger along what must be the railroad tracks to where I must live because it is away from the school, then taking my chin in my hand and staring some more, tapping my finger on my lips to see if this will help the map speak to me.

The sun is leaving and so I try to catch what I can of it, jumping from wood to wood between the iron lines. But one is too short and two is too long and so I try to walk beside the track on the rocks but this is worse. Me, I would rather the wood and so I go back to it and step short and quick.

Dark will come fast now and so I look for places to sleep as I leap from wood to wood, the smell of it making me dream hot summer and playing with my two nimiseyag near the tracks and the big shining water where we live. I will get home. I will. But the wind blows hard and cold at my back and I'm tired and I'm dreaming more than walking from wood to wood and my foot doesn't pay attention and doesn't make the step it needs to so that it catches wood instead and I can't stop from falling, my forehead cracking on the track.

Bright light like staring into sun and the little wait till the hurt explodes and I touch my head and my hand is red. Don't move. Just wait. Wait. The pain will go. My nose to tar wood and eyes to crushed rocks. Just wait. When I can push up and sit again, the wind howls with laughing.

Dizzy, me, walking now. It's time to find a place in the trees and use a match for a fire. Up ahead and then down the small hill of the tracks I see where amik lives, a beaver pond and beside it a stretch of trees that will help stop the wind. I know this will be a good spot. Fallen trees to hide in.

Close to the pond, amik slaps its fat tail to let the others know I've come. Another answers with a slap and the sound of water echoes. My father's nindede, my nimishomis, when he trapped amik in his snare, used to throw the tail on the fire until it bubbled and turned real black and then he peeled away the skin and ate the whole thing. He was the strongest man in the world, my nindede says, because this is what he ate. Oh, if only amik would give me his tail.

Cracking of dry twigs and handful of moss and the scrape of one match on rock and a little fire comes alive. I found a place, me, under gaawaandag spruce and I think I might be all right tonight. Fingers on my forehead. The bump is ever big but it's mostly stopped bleeding. I taste the bit of blood because there's nothing else to eat.

I pile sticks onto the fire and close my

eyes. So tired but cold and hungry won't
let me sleep too easy. Count backward
from that number five.

                    Naanan
                            Niiwin
                                    Niswi
                                            Niizh
                                            Bizhig
Then do it again.
                    Naanan
                            Niiwin
                                    Niswi
                                            Niizh
                                            Bizhig
Then do it again.
                    Naanan
                            Niiwin
                                    Niswi

Niizh

Bizhig

The slap of amik tail is the slap of
teacher across my face. The other children
stare at me. I spoke out loud in the class
in my tongue because I forgot what
Nindede warned me.

Nimaanendam! I say but it comes out
with my tongue not his. I mean to say I
am sorry, I say, and he slaps me again so I
fall out of my chair. I meant to say it in
English, I try to tell him, but my tongue
came out instead. I'm sorry, I say from the
floor. He thinks I make fun and he grips
my hair in his fist and drags me out the
room and down some stairs and to the
dark basement that scares us all to dying.
He takes the key from the metal ring on

his waist and he opens a door and pushes me in. I wait for him to close the door, tiny light and a skinny mattress on the floor covered in yellow stains.

Take off your clothes.

I shake.

He walks to me and his hand meets my face so I taste red. I remove my shirt. He waits. I remove my shoes. He waits. I remove my pantses. He waits then he picks them up and takes them away and locks the door.

Nothing I can do in the cold dark but shiver. Try not to cry. Please don't cry. Please. Daga. Afraid. Ningotaaj. Cold. Ningiikaj. I sleep. The door cries and I wake. Dark but he is a tall shadow staring down at me. He lies down beside me on the skinny mattress that smells of old pee

and he takes me in his arms and holds
me. His skin is gizhaate. Hot. His skin
glows like a fish belly in the dark.
Ozhaawaa. He pushes himself against me.
He smells like the colour called brown.
He pushes me on my stomach. His
mouth. Nindoon. On my back. Nipikwan.
Hurt. He hurts. Don't hurt me. Please
don't hurt.

SNOW GOOSE

The boy, Chanie, shakes as the first sleet
begins to fall that eve. He sleeps fitfully,
and in his dream the sleet that soaks him
is the sweat of the teacher pounding
above. His pathetic fire douses, and fat
and full we who have become a wood
tick extract tiny fangs from his calf and
take our time crawling out from the worn
pants of the boy. He will awake soon and
will experience the most miserable night

of his young existence, near frozen to death by a beaver pond, a small flock of snow geese come down from the skies to take watery respite from those that would hunt and eat them, their stark white-feathered bodies huddled in the black centre of the pond.

The beavers work through the darkest hours and pay no mind to the strange shivering human nearby. They know what awaits him, and there's nothing for them to do but ply the night till dawn, to chew through poplar and balsam and birch to stunt their teeth, to keep those teeth from growing so fast and long that the bottom ones will curve and eventually pierce the top of the skull if beaver were ever to turn lazy. They listen for breaks in the dam, the sound of flowing water as much an enemy as the prowling timber wolf nearby. The beaver family tenses to waddle as one back into their pond's safety when they hear the waking gasp of the boy, a cry of pain and of fear and, for the first time, the bawl of understanding what mortality means.

There's nothing for us to do now but watch the boy push himself up and into a crouch, thin arms wrapped about torso as sleet turns to snow then back to sleet again. His body temperature in the darkest hours of night drops as close to what a human can withstand before his system beckons coma to keep the sluggish blood pumping, extremities of the brown-skinned boy a sickly yellow white. We wait and witness the body quakes. The tremors. The quakes again. Blood pressure drops with temperature and our dark eyes refract no light. But as mornings must, this last one returns. Not with the sun but with a simper.

We watch as Chanie forces himself to a stand and stumbles away from the beaver pond and to the tracks to continue his slow walk. The sleet has stopped but the sky hangs thick with dark cloud, and a north wind is just beginning to sing in earnest. Chanie is right in remembering his family lives near the railroad tracks by big shining water, but what he does not fully understand is that home is hundreds of miles away.

Those of us who choose to become snow geese now rouse ourselves with our discordant song and pedal webbed feet to shore, scouring for a bit of sustenance to help us on our flight south. One of us pecks near where Chanie slept, roots out bits of green in the brown, eyes and pursues the engorged wood tick that tries to burrow under leaves, then swallows him with a satisfied click of beak before digging deeper for more.

Lead goose in pond lifts and ruffles wings. Time to fly to beat more coming weather, and so she pushes hard with webbed feet and commands wings to pound the air, neck pointed straight in the direction she must go until she begins her lift, webbed feet now running across water as wings work harder and she catches a small draft that lifts her up above the spruce and poplar and Precambrian spine as ancient as the world, the others following, none wanting to be

left behind, until we form a V in the air
and allow long white flight feathers
their work.

We peer down at the boy, a dark speck
on the tracks below, honking out a
greeting to him, letting him know we see
him, that we witness his lonely walk
now a torture. As we follow the tracks
that cut through rock and muskeg and
bush we talk back and forth among
ourselves about how far we think the
boy can go before his body fails. Not far.
Our shining eyes catch the day's low
light and we can see how these tracks we
follow from above stretch impossibly
across the harsh earth. For all the chance
he has we might as well try to fly to the
near-full moon that plans to appear, if
only briefly, tonight.

We honk a few more greetings and garbled words of encouragement to the boy before veering away from the tracks and south to where we, at least those of us who survive the journey, will find a bit of warmth. There won't be any more warmth for young Chanie until he meets the last of us late tonight.

RABBIT

I can see more bad weather coming.
Walking has made me a bit warmer but
my clothes are wet. Nindede would tell
me to get them dry now and build a
shelter till I can feel a bit stronger again.
But everything is so wet. Gaawiin. No.
My map. I reach into my pocket and can
feel it tear when I touch it. Gentle. Stop.
Take shaking hand and try to take map
out proper. It tears I shake so hard. It's
ruined. Gaawiin.

Ever stupid, me! Ever stupid! Why
didn't I roll it up in the small glass jar
with the matches? I reach my hand in my
pocket and squish the map with my fist.
Water between fingers. I take it out and
open my fist. I stare. This is their map.
This is not mine. My map is this wood
and the two lines and my map is walking
till I'm home. I don't need their stupid
map. I throw it like a ball and the wind
from giiwedinong takes it to it, to the
north, and like I asked it to happen, snow
starts coming down. Build a fire now, I
hear Nindede say.

A dead tree down the small hill.
Breaking of twigs but no dry moss and
then I remember the paper that wrapped
the meat of mooz. It feels dry. Water drips
off it when I take it from my pocket. I

squeeze the paper in a ball and lean over it and take out the match jar and then a match and I light it on my zipper and my lean stops the snow from falling on it. Touch match to paper but paper doesn't want to. Just turns green for a bit and then smoky. Second match. Second light. Paper's ugly. It won't take fire into it. Four matches left. Then three. Stop. Save them. Walk to get warm. I can feel me getting slow. I must get up. So cold and yet my body doesn't want to move. Move.

Then I see it staring at me just a few feet away. It's been staring at me for how long? Waabooz. Big ears up and brown fur already beginning to turn its winter white. Long feet ready to jump it away. We look at eyes for a while. I never knew this feeling before. Waabooz the rabbit

isn't scared of me. Waabooz looks sad.
The snow falls in little hisses in the trees
and we look at each other and there is no
more fear. Waabooz finally turns and
jumps slow away.

On the tracks I fall one time. Bizhig.
Two times. Niizh. Three. Niswi. I don't
feel the hurting anymore. The snow stops
and starts and stops. The day becomes
afternoon becomes darker becomes dark.
I slow walk. Ever slow. One wood. Two
woods. Three. I fall again and try so hard
to push back up.

My hands shake as I step into night.
Nindede and me, we once checked our
snare to find waabooz so new in it that
his long hands and feet still shaked like
mine do now. I try to imagine being
him, wearing his brown fur turning

white. I shake.

Above me the clouds tear open to the moon. It's almost full. I can't stop now or I won't get up. My feet work slow and I look at moon when I can. Everything so heavy. Shaky. Slow. Feet work. Feet please work. Feet. Ninzidan.

Ninzidan drag and the sky spins and moon smiles at me and I'm falling. Oh. Hurt. On my back. My front. My back. My front. My back. Beside the tracks. Moon above me smiles. Hands and feet shake. White breath. So cold. Ever cold. Nindede taught me how to find north. I hear him say it. Gimik-wenden-ina, Chanie? Do you remember? I do, Nin-dede. That star. Anang.

They're watching me from the edge of the bush. I can tell. They been following me since the school went away from me. Me from it. What's the word for them, for what follows me, Nindede?

Manitous. No English word for that. Where are you going, Chanie? Nindede asks. He looks so sad. Aandi ezhaayan? Where are you going?

I'm going to go, me. Giiwe. Home.

My hands shake and my feet shake and there is no more getting up. I am waabooz in his snare. I shake. Shake. Think your words. Speak your words. Head. Nishtigwaan. Cold. Gisinaa. Warm. Ningiizhooz. No. Gaawiin. Yes. Eya'. Nose. Injaanzh. Eye. Nishkiizhig.

Father. Nindede. Heart. Ninde'. Father. Nindede. Heart. Ninde'. Father. Nindede. Heart. Ninde'. Father. Heart. Nindede. Ninde'. Nnnnnnn.

LYNX

We follow Chanie all day on our great
slippered feet of fur, stopping once to
pounce on the slowest snow goose as the
small flock lands for afternoon rest, and
again for a quick chase of snowshoe hare
dazed by what it saw in the young boy's
eyes. Today is not a difficult one, if only
in the sense that we don't feel challenged
by what we stalk. Boy's step is so slow it
makes us lazy, our pursuit of prey one of

boredom more so than need.

As dusk becomes night, Chanie shaking and stumbling and weakened by cold and hunger, we pay special attention. The time for us to act is near. He summons the hare to let us know that soon he will be ready for the lynx's embrace. Rabbit is our favourite sustenance, after all.

And when he stumbles and falls along the slick steel of tracks, the near-full moon splitting open the clouds above, we watch with yellow eyes, retinas glittering in that orb's light, young Chanie roll down the embankment of rocks and then stare up at our brethren that inhabit the sky.

We watch his breath slow, white in the darkness as he speaks his words, those words born alive, tangible in his frozen puffs. Hot moisture of breath meeting the

freeze become signals to the world that
Chanie is still here.

And then with a shiver, a kick,
he's gone.

We must move quick, for great actor
brother moon begins his final call before
night's curtain is drawn, the clouds who
will soon envelop him beginning their
skitter. Wary, we leave the cover of trees
and the perch from where we watch.

We who choose so become the mother,
this greatest of the lynx, her shadow so
large in waning moonlight that even the
best two-legged hunter grown strong on
beaver's rich tail would shake in fear if he
were to witness her slink toward the boy.
The little warmth left in the child crystal-
lizes on his lips and our twitching nose
lowers to breathe in the scent. Long and

rough tongue licks his whitening cheek, his ears, his forehead, his eyes.

And now as cloud curtains shut on this lonely performance, moon bowing to the darkness, a snowstorm squalls through the cut rock of tracks, covering a country's shield where Chanie lies, great lynx protective above him.

We watch as the lynx through a thickening screen of snow stands up on her hind legs to look down upon the child. She reaches her long arms to take him in her paws and then lifts him up and into her embrace. As the snow falls thicker, she wraps him more tightly to her so that he may feel again, and with the first true snow of the season falling now, whipped by the wind through the canyon cut out of rock, the mother lynx waltzes

Chanie warm in her fur-clad arms and into the forest, away from the tracks.

We watch patient as day breaks clear and cold, snow melting when sun rises higher so that by early afternoon when the thundering chug of an approaching train sounds, Chanie's still body is exposed. The engineer slows as much as he's able and stares down upon the frozen Indian boy just feet from the tracks. He radios the sad find in and pushes the engine to speed again.

Hours later, a few pale authorities arrive to snap pictures and collect the body. They note in photographs how the boy lies upon his back, his thin clothing soaked, his feet turned inward, not out. They find little in his pockets except a handful of chewed red willow twigs along with a small screw-top jar containing a few wooden matches. When the little they can collect is collected, they roll the body into a sheet and begin the trouble of carrying it out. And when it's convenient, which turns out to be weeks later, their notification to the deceased's family will be the return of said deceased in a thin casket, remains enclosed, back to his people and to his home.

In the forest, we dance in a great oval that contracts and expands as breath draws in, draws out. Owl and mouse and wood tick, rabbit and pike and beaver. Hummingbird, crow, snow goose and spider. Mother lynx and Chanie we call to the centre to honour proper, and we revel in the world we've created around them. Sun rises to test the moon and moon rises to rest the sun. And still we watch. We watch the boy warm in our presence, watch him dance and eat and share his shy smile, his dark eyes turned darker and sparkling.

The real-life Chanie "Charlie" Wenjack was forcibly taken from his parents and his sisters and his home in Ogoki Post, Northern Ontario, in 1964 when he was nine years old. He asked his sisters to please look after his two beloved dogs until he returned from Cecilia Jeffrey Indian Residential School over six hundred kilometres away in Kenora. None of them knew how long he'd be gone. Chanie came home two years later in a casket.

Chanie wasn't, by a very long shot, the only child to leave for residential school and never return. Many thousands of children died during their time in these alien institutions—from disease, from abuse, from exposure or accidents while trying to run away. The true number of children who died under the watch of those responsible for their care will never be known. Proper records were purposefully not kept. The death of these countless innocents remains one of the deepest, most brutal stains on Canada's history. More than six thousand dead children's names have so far been uncovered, but there are thought to be far, far more, many of them buried in unmarked graves near the residential schools that pocked our country.

From the 1870s until 1996, when the last school closed its doors, more than 150,000

Indigenous children over seven generations were removed from their families in an attempted cultural genocide. Chanie, for me and for a number of others, has become a symbol not just of this tragedy but of the resilience of our First Nations, Inuit and Métis people—which is why I use the word "attempted." Our cultures were forced underground for a long time, but they have re-emerged despite the odds. And they are thriving once more.

Ian Adams wrote "The Lonely Death of Charlie Wenjack" for *Maclean's* not long after Chanie's tragic death in 1966; up to that point, it was one of the few times that a national publication had exposed this dark national secret. And Chanie Wenjack couldn't have known it, but that sweet boy forced the first public inquiry into residential schools in

Canada. At the conclusion of this inquiry, the all-white jury unanimously questioned not just the philosophy but also the morality behind residential schools . . . although it would take another thirty years for the last institution's doors to be shut.

It will take many more years before the intergenerational trauma left in the wake of this grotesque social experiment begins to abate. The Truth and Reconciliation Commission worked tirelessly for many years to uncover the truth—and now the tougher part, the reconciliation, begins.